# PHANTOM OF THE WATER PARK

WRITTEN AND ILLUSTRATED BY KIRK SCROGGS

DAMP WITH TERROR!

LITTLE, BROWN AND COMPANY
Books for Young Readers
New York Boston

Special Thanks to:
Steve Deline, Jackie Greed, Mark Mayes, Hiland Hall, Alejandra, Inge Govaerts, Suppasak Viboonlarp, Joe Kocian, Jim Jeong, Hickelbee's, Amy Wilson, Andrea, Jill, Ames, Alison, Elizabeth, Saho, Maria, and the Little, Brown Crew—yahoo!!

A wet and wild thanks to Ashley & Carolyn Grayson, Dav Pilkey, Christa and Andrea and the Mrs. Nelson's Books crew, and Helen Coronato.

And an extra wrinkled waterlogged thanks to Mamacita, Corey and Candace, and Harold Aulds.



Little, Brown and Company

Hachette Book Group USA
237 Park Avenue, New York, NY 10017
Visit our Web site at www.lb-kids.com

First Edition: May 2008

ISBN-13: 978-0-316-00687-3 / ISBN-10: 0-316-00687-4

10 9 8 7 6 5 4 3 2 1

CW

Printed in the United States of America

Series design by Saho Fujii

The illustrations for this book were done in Staedtler ink on Canson Marker paper, then digitized with Adobe Photoshop for color and shade. The text was set in Humana Sans Light and the display type was handlettered.

# CHAPTERS

CHAPTER 1

# Beat the Heat

Ladies and gentlemen, thrill seekers from all over the globe and parts of Iowa . . . step right up and brave the most terrifying water ride this side of a broken fire hydrant. You'll plummet down steep drops, hit speeds guaranteed to make you hurl, and land face-first into a churning pool of frothy water and oily suntan lotion residue.

Hold on to your swim trunks!

# YEE HAW!

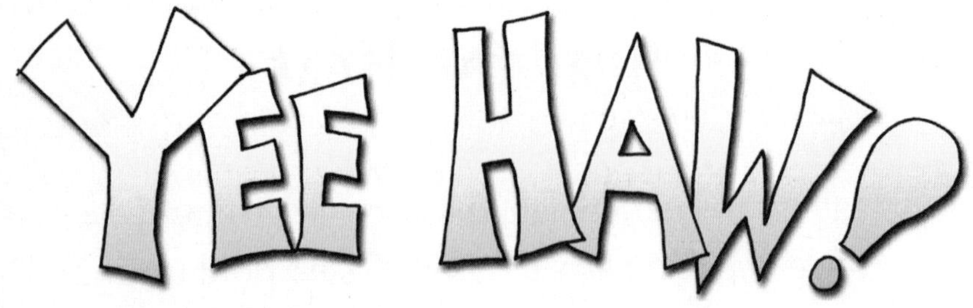

The water is rougher than expected! Notice the way it winds wildly around the craggy curves and through the rocky crevices.

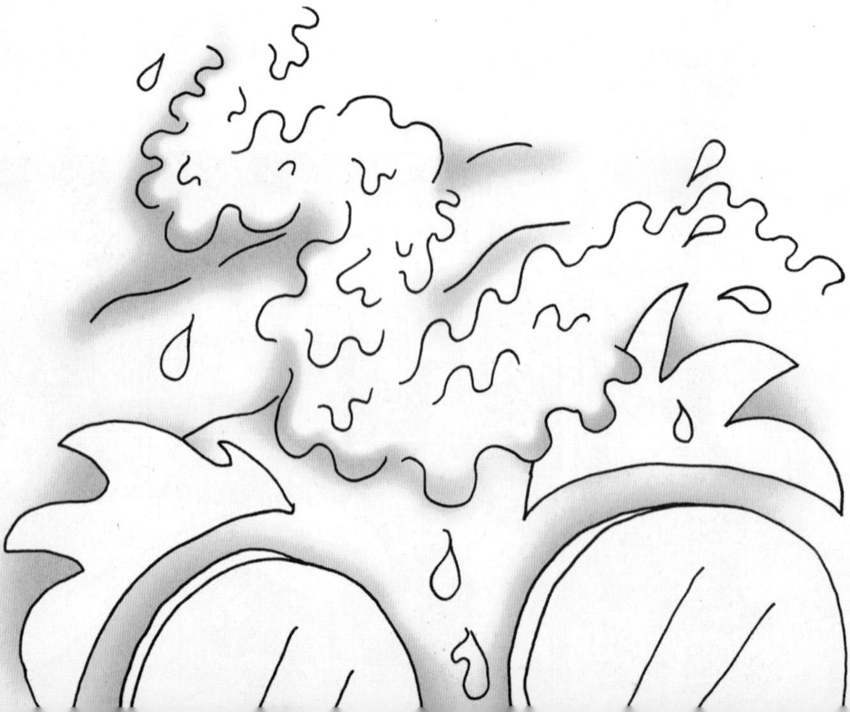

Wait a minute! Those are just rivers of sweat running down Grampa's wrinkly forehead. You see, a horrible heat wave had hit Gingham County and it had forced Grampa to sit around in his underwear all day—actually, he does that anyway.

It was so hot that Gramma had to cool off Paco the goldfish's bowl with ice cubes.

Merle was forced to eat fish-flavored ice cream instead of his usual Kitty Kutlets cat food.

Jubal and I tried to play in the sprinkler, but all that came out was hot steam.

"This is hopeless," I said.

"Oh well," said Jubal. "At least I can use this opportunity to steam some veggies."

"I give up," said Grampa. "The AC's not workin', it's a hundred and three degrees in the shade, and my butt's stuck to the chair. It's so hot, the jalapeños are complaining! I think I'm just gonna melt into a big puddle of goo right here."

"Oooh!" said Gramma. "Then I'd better go get the mop."

CHAPTER 2

# Emergency Blues Flash!

The news wasn't getting any better.

"Hi, folks! This is Blue Norther coming to you live in leopard print bikini briefs. Why, you ask? Cuz it's hotter than habanero horseradish, that's why. Officials say there's a shortage of drinking water, and local 7-Elevens say they're desperately low on blue raspberry Slurpees. Have a wonderful day!"

Then our prayers were answered. We saw an amazing, tantalizing, exhilarating commercial for Gingham County's best water park, Castle Waterhösen.

The park's owner, Dame Judy Drenched, invited everyone to come: "We strive to bring you the most terrifying, gut-wrenchingly extreme rides guaranteed to turn you white with fright. Bring the children!"

"That's it!" I yelled. "That's how we'll beat the heat. At Castle Waterhösen."

"And looky!" said Gramma. "There's a coupon in the paper. If we bring five empty Pork Cracklins bags we get in for half price."

CHAPTER 3

# Kersplashic Park

So, we managed to find a few empty bags of Pork Cracklins and headed for our wet wonderland.

"Ooh! Ooh!" I said. "I think I can see it!"

And there it was. Castle Waterhösen—forty acres of liquid fun.

"I can smell the chlorine and the funnel cakes already," said Grampa.

After waiting in a ridiculously long line, we were let in to the park—except for Merle. There was a strict "No Cat" policy, which was a shame because Merle was dying to try out his new bathing suit.

First we posed for a photo with Mildred the Merpig, Castle Waterhösen's beloved mascot.

They even printed the pic on a coffee mug for just $28.50.

We checked out the map of the park to figure out what to ride first.

"Let's start out with something simple and work our way up to insanely bonkers," said Grampa.

CHAPTER 4

# The River Mild

We got off to a dull start on the least exciting ride ever, Old Man River.

"Grampa," I said, "this ride's about as thrilling as a nap on a rainy day."

"I think it's relaxing," said Grampa. "Besides, your Gramma can't take anything too scary. She's very delicate."

"Delicate my patooty!" yelled Gramma. "I came here for some extreme thrills! Now get up off that lazy river and let's go hit some waves!"

"Righteous!" said Grampa.

"Hot diggity dog! Let's go!" I said as we reached for our beach towels to dry off.

“Wait a minute!” I said. “That’s not a beach towel. Grampa, you’re drying your butt with Merle!”

“I thought something felt a little whiskery back there,” said Grampa.

“It was me,” said Gramma. “I just couldn’t leave Merle outside so I snuck him in disguised as a beach towel. Please don’t report me to the authorities!”

“I’ll think about it,” said Grampa.

CHAPTER 5

# Now That's More Like It!

So, Merle joined us on some pretty killer rides like the thrilling Runaway Spitwad.

The dizzying Spin Cycle, which turned out to be good, clean fun.

The simple, yet effective, Big Hose Down.

And the zesty Chili Dog Derby, flowing with actual three-alarm chili.

"Next stop, Hammerhead Mountain," I said. "Sixteen stories of tube chutes, jagged rocks, and robot sharks."

"It looks so inviting," said Grampa.

"All right," said Grampa as we got in. "This ride is extremely intense and terrifying and probably dangerous. There's a good chance you could lose a leg or possibly an earlobe. Granny, you go first."

We shot down the chute at warp speed. It was awesome!

"Weeeeeee!!!" said Gramma.

"I hate to spoil the party," said Jubal, "but look behind us!"

A humongous hammerhead shark was breathing right down my neck!

"I don't want to alarm anyone," I said, "but you might want to start paddling. Fast!"

“Don’t worry, Wiley!” said Grampa, spinning around. “It’s just a mechanical shark. Those aren’t real shark teeth. They’re just razor-sharp steel replicas. These robots are programmed not to harm the guests. Look, I’ll put my feet in his mouth.”

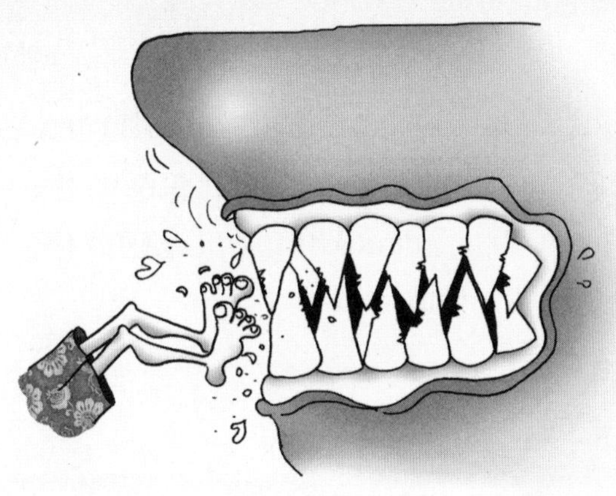

Suddenly, the jaws of the shark slammed shut, just nipping Grampa's toes!

"I'm all right!" said Grampa. "I needed a good toenail clipping anyway."

The robo shark kept coming!

"Look!" I yelled. "Up there on that rock shaped like a crab eating a chili burger. That guy in the mask and cheap Dracula outfit is operating the shark by remote control."

We had to stop the shark ourselves. Jubal and I shoved our tubes into the hammerhead's mouth.

"Quick, Merle!" I said. "These tubes are deflating fast!"

Merle used his famous cat-snorkeling skills to swim under the belly of the beast and his superior mechanical skills to deactivate it.

We spilled out into the pool at the bottom of the mountain, dead robot and all.

"Let's ride it again!" shouted Gramma.

Park owner, Dame Judy Drenched, showed up to inspect the faulty shark.

"We regret any harm our malfunctioning sharks may have caused. Anyone who may have lost a limb or a relative shall receive a coupon for a free order of seasoned curly fries at our Supreme Food Court."

"Seasoned curly fries," said Grampa. "Now that's customer service!"

CHAPTER 6

# Wet and Weird

"Stay alert, Jubal," I said. "Keep your eyes peeled for that shadowy figure. There's something strange afoot. Even stranger than Grampa."

"That's pretty strange," said Jubal.

On our way to the next ride, we ran into Nate Farkles, Gingham's finest veterinarian.

"G'day, Nate!" I said. "Hey, why don't you join us on our next terrifying ride?"

"Why not?" said Nate. "Let me just drop off the kiddos first."

CHAPTER 7

# Snot so Fast

Next stop, the Nasal Drop, where riders plunge twenty feet from the schnoz of an authentic Easter Island statue.

"We can choose between three different nose speeds," I said, "sniffles, sneezy, or snot blasters."

"Hey, you guys pick the nose and I'll get in it," said Grampa.

Gramma went on the more advanced snot blaster while we went on the sniffler.

"Who knew a runny nose could be this fun?" said Jubal.

Then it was Grampa's and Nate's turn.

But there was a problem in the left nostril. Grampa and Nate went in, but nothing came out! We heard a loud scream from deep within the nostril.

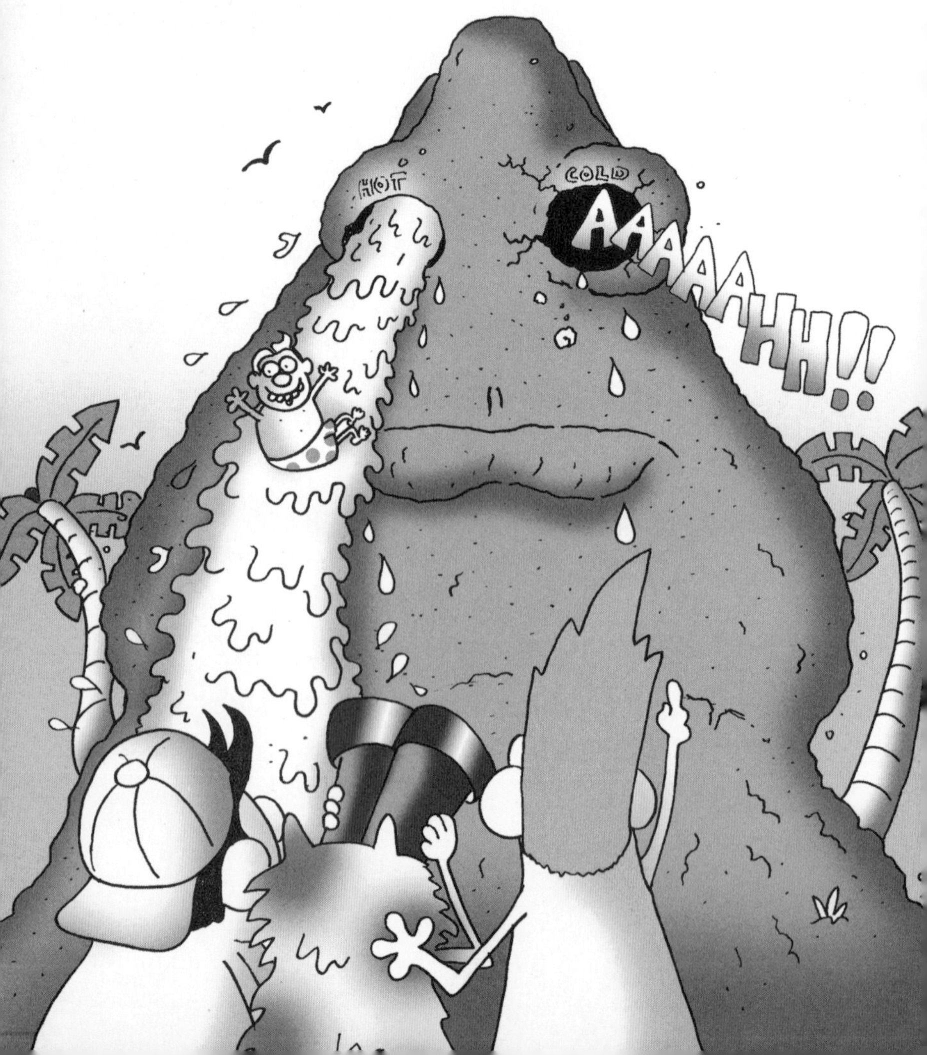

Rescue teams swooped in with heavy-duty tissues and a King Kong–size bottle of nose spray.

Finally, the blocked nostril gave way and Grampa came flying out with the fury of a sneezing water buffalo.

CHAPTER 8

# Nothing to See Here

Grampa was on his back and beside him was a strange lollipop that must have fallen out of the nose.

"Grampa!" I said. "Are you okay? What happened?"

"It was horrible!" said Grampa dramatically.

"Nate and I were zooming through the nostril laughing and singing the theme to *Scooby Doo*.

"That's when we spotted that pint-sized punk blocking our way. He smelled like lollipops and corned beef.

"Nate vanished and I hung on to a nose hair for dear life. The next thing I can remember is lying here on my back."

Once again, Dame Judy Drenched showed up.

"We apologize for your missing friend," she said. "Please accept this coupon for a free cinnamon sugar churro."

"Churro?!" I said. "Lady, you've got a phantom on the loose, killer robot sharks, and a faulty schnoz. You've gotta close down this park!"

"Did she say cinnamon sugar?" asked Grampa.

"Don't worry, my precious loved ones," said Grampa. "Dame Drenched might not seem to care, but I won't stand for it. I will not rest until we uncover this phantom menace and find Nate Farkles. Now, let's go get some fried pickles and jalapeño corn dogs."

CHAPTER 9

# Hans Solo

Near the concession stand, we spotted something even more terrifying than the phantom.

"Ooh!" squealed Gramma with delight. "The salsa supershow is starting in five minutes!"

"Oh, joy," I moaned. "No small boy should have to see an amusement park musical show. It's child abuse!"

The director of the show was Hans Lotion and his grandson, Jurg—hey, wait a minute! His grandson, Jurgen, was nowhere to be found. That was pretty weird.

"Good afternoon, ladies and gentlemen," said Hans. "Velcome to ze show. I hope you brought your boogie shoes because ve are going to tear ze roof off zis hizzy!"

The Big Hair Sugar Sisters came out hula hooping with shiny mirrored inner tubes to sing their opening number, "Undersea Salsa Shakedown".

"Let's get outta here before I get seasick," said Grampa.

So we left Gramma to enjoy the show and headed over to the most terrifying ride ever. . . .

CHAPTER 10

# Creature from the Nacho Cheese Lagoon

"The Nacho Xtreme!" I said. "Where we'll ride giant tortilla chips down a mountain on rivers of actual nacho cheese."

"You had me at nacho cheese," said Grampa.

The ride was cheese-tastic! We shot through canyons of corn chips on a torrent of white-water queso.

"Isn't this awesome?" I said.

"Uhmm hmmmm yummmh!" said Grampa. Don't ask me what that means—his mouth was full of nacho cheese.

That's when it happened. The dreaded phantom floated by on a giant jalapeño.

"Look out!" I yelled. "We've got company."

But before I could make a move, a giant claw came up out of the cheese!

Out popped a creature that was half human/ half crawdad/all ugly!

"I don't know what it is," said Grampa, "but I bet it'd taste delicious with some melted butter and proper seasoning."

I managed to temporarily blind the beast with a squirt of super-spicy jalapeño juice.

Jubal did a leaping Muenster Cheese Missile Kick, but he missed and nailed Fran Calhoon's monster hairdo instead.

Grampa scared the crawdad with a jar of premium tartar sauce (sworn enemy of all things fishy).

Merle challenged the karate crayfish to a monster catfight.

CHAPTER 11

# Salsa Y Queso

Merle and the monster battled so fiercely that they formed a giant cheese ball that rolled down the mountain of corn chips and landed smack dab on the stage, right in the middle of "Besame Mucho"!

Mildred the Merpig jumped up onstage and did a quick flamenco number with the crawdad and his crab claw castanets.

"We can't work like this!" yelled the Sugar Sisters. "We're being upstaged by a samba-lovin' shrimp in flip-flops!"

Then the beast ran off with Merle.

CHAPTER 12

# Catnapped!

"We've gotta get Merle! He's been swiped!" I yelled.

"All right, but first I need to stop by Pepty Bizmo Peak," said Grampa, clutching his belly. "I ate too much nacho cheese."

"Okay," I said. "To find Merle we've got to examine the clues and retrace our steps. Jubal, write this down—it's very important. First, there was the mystery lollipop just like the kind Jurgen eats. Then, Jurgen was mysteriously missing during the nightmare musical number. I smell a rat and I think that rat's name is Jurgen!"

"Actually, there's a rat standing behind you," said Jubal.

"Quick!" I said. "Let's look at that photo on the mug again. Just as I thought. Hans and Jurgen are entering a secret hatch in the background. Does anyone remember where that hatch is?"

"Wiley, I can't even remember what I ate for breakfast this morning," said Grampa.

"Well," said Gramma, "luckily, I snuck in our prized bloodhounds disguised as Swedish tourists."

"You snuck in Esther and Chavez?" Grampa asked.

"Shhhh! Today, they're Inga and Ulrich," whispered Gramma. "I just couldn't leave them in that hot yard all day."

We let Esther—I mean Inga—sniff the mystery lollipop.

Ulrich closely examined the coffee mug.

Then they led us on a grand journey of sniffing and snooping and occasional scratching.

CHAPTER 13

# Sweet and Sewer Chicken

Inga and Ulrich located the secret hatchway, and they guarded the entrance while we went inside.

"I can't believe we're crawling into the rear end of a giant chicken," said Jubal.

"Don't say I never took you anywhere," said Grampa.

We dropped down into the sewer system beneath Castle Waterhösen. It was cold, drippy, slimy, and smelled like a grizzly bear's underwear.

"This place is gross," I said.

"Oh, I don't know," said Grampa. "If you add a few pillows, some throw rugs, and a few scented candles, it'd make a lovely room for zombies or rabid rodents."

Suddenly, we spotted a bunch of tiny little beady eyes peering out at us from the darkness.

"Don't be scared," said Grampa. "Those are probably just the eyes of hundreds of vampire bats just looking for a light snack."

"Those aren't bats," I said, "they're beavers. And they're clutching one of Merle's hair balls! Where did you get that hair ball, little guy?"

"They can't understand you, Wiley," said Grampa. "Beavers communicate by beating their tails against a tough, solid surface like the ground, a tree trunk, or one of your Gramma's homemade pork chops."

So, I grabbed a log and beat it on the floor seventeen times. "I'm using Morse code to ask him where Merle is," I said.

The beaver smacked his tail on the ground thirty-two times, which translated to, "Sure. Walk this way, homeslice."

We followed the beavers down a long corridor.

We found Merle in a huge chamber, on an operating table surrounded by crawdad monsters.

"Oh, no! They're performing horrible experiments on Merle!" I said.

"No, wait," said Gramma. "That one is giving Merle a checkup. He's taking Merle's blood pressure just like a veterinarian would. Why, I think that crawdad is really—"

"Nate Farkles! Yes! It's true." It was Hans Lotion and his grandson, Jurgen (aka The Phantom of the Water Park). "Please excuse ze mess. Zis place may smell like raw sewage but ze rent is cheap and zey allow pets.

"It is here, underground, zat I have perfected a vay to transform any beast into a crawdad."

"Now why would you wanna go and turn a perfectly good veterinarian like Nate into a crawdad?" asked Grampa.

"Hee! Hee!" laughed Hans. "It is all part of our master plan to get revenge on Castle Vaterhösen for vhat zey did to my Jurgen."

CHAPTER 14

# Blue Moon

"It vas a long, long, long, long time ago. Actually, it vas last summer. Ve came to Castle Vaterhösen for some fun in ze sun. Jurgen brought his little friend, Penelope. Zey vere so cute you could just pinch zem.

"Jurgen vas riding ze vaterpark's steepest, scariest ride, Dead Dog Drop.

"Zat's vhen it happened. Jurgen vas going so fast zat his svimsuit blew right off. Ze poor little guy vas just in his birthday suit.

"Everyvone laughed at him. Hee! Hee! Actually, it is pretty funny now zat I zink about it. Jurgen hasn't spoken a vord since and he's never shown his tushy in public again, vhich is good because zere are laws against zat kind of zing.

"Now, Jurgen has sworn he vill have his revenge by ruining Castle Vaterhösen and turning everyone into half-human/half-crawdad mutants. It is his dream."

"Well, I guess it's good to have goals," said Grampa.

"But how?" I asked. "How do you turn someone into a crawdad? I've been trying for years and it never seems to work."

CHAPTER 15

# Craw Shucks!

"I present you ze greatest invention since ze Pop-Tart, ze **C**rawdad **R**estructuring **U**ltrasonic **D**evice, or **C.R.U.D.** for short. It is made of several common household items: a hula hoop, a nine-volt battery, a crawdad , and vone plutonium thermosonic reconfibulator."

"Oh yeah," said Grampa. "I think I have one of those out in the garage."

"Any creature zat passes through ze hoop vill be combined vith a crawdad. Look, I vill demonstrate vith zis duck."

Hans's duck jumped through the electrified hoop and came out the other side a mutant freak!

"He is now half crawdad/half duck. I shall call him Crawduck. Later, ve vill make a Crawdog and, if ve have time, a Crawdonkey.

"Ve can access any part of ze park through zese underground tunnels. Zat is how ve kidnapped Nate. Ve have also placed a giant C.R.U.D. device in ze latest attraction zat is opening in just ten minutes. Anyvone who gets on zat ride vill come out feeling a little . . . **crabby.** Hee hee!"

Hans tied us up and walked over to his monitor. "Before ve leave, I have a special torture in store for you."

"Oh, no," said Grampa. "You're gonna hook up a car battery to our pinky toes and put fire ants in our drawers, aren't you?"

"Nooo, hee hee!" said Hans. "I have somezing much vorse—you vill vatch zis video of *Barney's Christmas Miracle* on continuous repeat."

"I'll take the fire ants," said Jubal.

Hans and Jurgen took off to terrorize the park and left us with the crawdads.

"Merle!" I said. "Use your tail to summon the beavers to come gnaw through these ropes. Do it quick, before Barney sings 'I'm Dreaming of a Purple Christmas'!"

Merle started beating his tail frantically.

But the beavers were being held back by the evil Crawduck who was taunting them with his giant claws and terrible celery-and-peanut-butter breath.

"I guess we'll have to save ourselves," I said.

CHAPTER 16

# Give Yourself a Hand

Grampa managed to free one of his hands. "Help me scoot over to that electric hula hoop."

"Grampa!" I yelled as he reached for the **C.R.U.D.** "Don't do it! That's your bowling hand!"

But Grampa stuck it through the hoop anyway. "Aaaaaaaaahhh!!" he screamed. "It tickles!"

Grampa sported a fancy new crawdad claw that cut through the ropes with ease.

And opening stubborn pickle jars was a cinch!

"Go on without me!" Grampa said, fighting off the crawdads with his claw as we made our escape.

"We won't leave you!" I yelled.

"Be brave!" Grampa said. "And tell your Gramma that, despite her terrible casseroles, I love her!"

"I'm right here!" said Gramma angrily.

"Oh, yeah," said Grampa.

So, Gramma led the way as we burst out of the sewers and raced toward the grand opening of the mystery ride. If we were going to make it, we had to take a shortcut through the park.

We crossed the Zipper Zapper, which Hans and Jurgen had filled with real electric eels.

Then we jumped across Hot Rockin' River, which was now flowing with actual molten lava!

Then we stopped off for Hawaiian shaved ice, but the phantom had replaced the fruity syrup with prune juice. Jubal found this strangely delicious.

CHAPTER 17

# Get This Potty Started

We finally arrived at the new ride, a five-story toilet! Dame Drenched stood at the top and addressed the crowd.

"We are proud to present the latest in quality family entertainment. I give you Mount Flushmore."

We raced to the top just in the nick of time.

"Wait!" I yelled. "You can't let people on this ride! The phantom has placed a giant C.R.U.D. at the bottom of this toilet. Anyone who rides it will come out looking like an Alaskan king crab!"

"Smashing!" said Dame Drenched.

All of a sudden, Hans and Jurgen jumped out and pushed us all into the swirling johnny!

"Enjoy your svim!" said Hans.

## CHAPTER 18

# The Royal Flush

We swirled toward the bottom of the toilet at lightning speed.

"Well, this is it," I said. "Maybe it won't be so bad being half crawdad. We'll be unbeatable at arm wrestling and we'll never need to buy another nutcracker again."

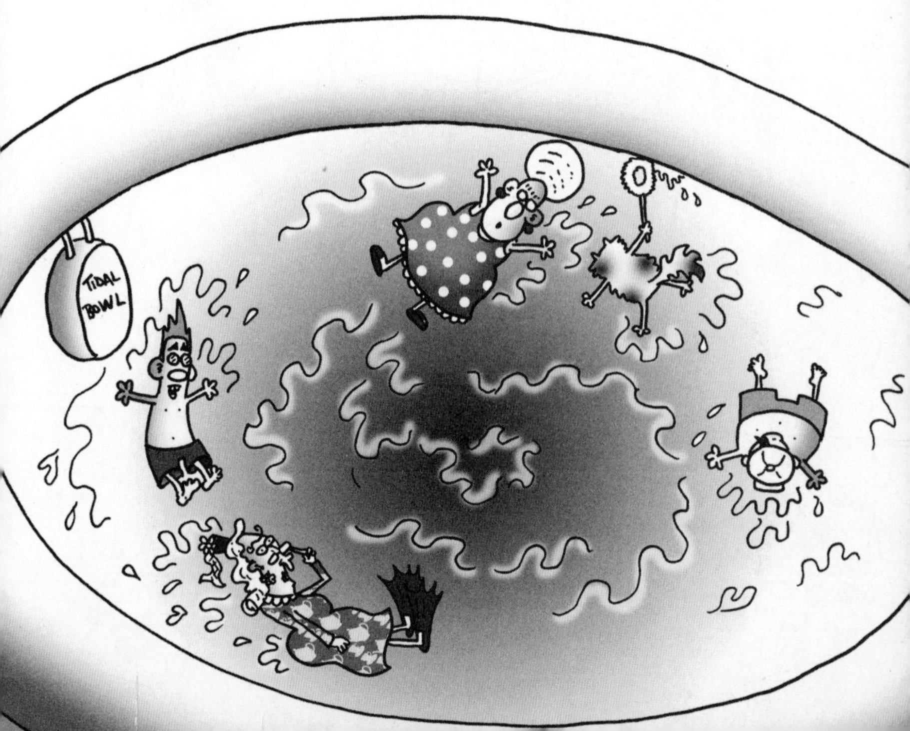

When we reached the bottom, Grampa and his beaver friends had blocked the drain with a giant beaver dam!

"How did you get to the bottom of the toilet before we did?" I asked.

"We came in through the rear!" said Grampa.

"Very clever!" Hans yelled from the rim. "Your vell-placed logjam has spoiled our party. Unfortunately, I forgot to bring my king-size plunger. So, instead, I vill crank up ze flow to full blast and turn zis toilet bowl into a fishbowl."

"Speaking of fishes!" said Gramma. "I brought us a secret weapon!" Gramma pulled Paco's fishbowl out of her big hair! "I just couldn't leave him in that hot house all day."

"Swim, young Paco," Gramma said, releasing him into the rushing water. "Turn off that valve, fulfill your destiny!"

Most people don't know this, but Paco's daddy was an Atlantic salmon and jumping upstream was his specialty.

Paco swam all the way up the raging current and shut off the valve.

CHAPTER 19

# Put Your Hans Up

Water park police swooped in on Hans and Jurgen, but they had one more trick up their sleeves.

"Just thought you should know, ve have activated ze self-destruct button on ze **C.R.U.D.**," said Hans. "In exactly thirty seconds, zis potty gonna go boom! Hee hee!"

"You hear that, Grampa?" I said. "This baño's gonna blow any second!"

"I guess it's time for my Creole Commode-Cracker Chop!" said Grampa.

Grampa used all of his might and chopped the porcelain bowl. It shattered and we all jumped through the hole.

We managed to escape just as the **C.R.U.D.** exploded!

"The toilet's launching into the sky!" I yelled.

"Darn! I should have used it when I had the chance!" said Grampa.

Russian cosmonauts reported seeing the latrine launch from outer space.

Back on Earth, our troubles were not over yet. The crawdad monsters attacked and Jubal was holding them off with Dippy Dots ice cream pellets.

"Hans!" I yelled. "Tell us how to transform them back into humans and er . . . ducks."

"Vhy vould I tell you?" said Hans.

"Because if you don't, Grampa will sing every song from *The Sound of Music*, karaoke-style, while I eat a whole box of delicious peanut buttery Spudscout cookies without even giving you a bite."

"I don't care," said Hans nervously. "Enjoy your silly cookies."

"Mmm!" I said, smearing chocolate all over my face. "I like to eat three at a time, like a big chocolatey peanut butter sandwich, then I wash it down with some ice-cold glistening milk."

"Okay! Okay!" screamed Hans. "You people are so cruel! I'll tell you how to change zem back. Zeir bodies are unstable. If you submerge zem in salty vater zat is above eighty-five degrees, zey vill change back. Now, give me a cookie."

"Where are we gonna find that much warm, salty water?" Jubal asked.

## CHAPTER 20

# A Warm Welcome

"To the kiddie pool!" I yelled. For some weird reason, the water in the kiddie pool is always salty and over eighty-five degrees.

"Grampa! Get in and lure the crawdads into the water!"

Grampa got in and, sure enough, his hand changed back to its normal, bony self.

"Hey, crawdads!" Grampa yelled at the monsters. "Your mama eats barnacles off a beluga's belly!"

"That's cold," said Jubal.

The angered crawdads jumped into the water and began to vibrate. Within seconds, they were transformed into their old selves.

"Boy! It's great to be back to normal," said Nate, "but I sure am gonna miss that tough, spiny exoskeleton."

CHAPTER 21

# How Could You Be So Shellfish?

Despite their diabolical plans, Dame Drenched was moved by Hans's and Jurgen's tale of his lost bathing suit.

"I hereby apologize for your traumatic experience at our park," said Drenched. "I now present to you this forty-ounce Castle Waterhösen collector's cup filled with a tasty carbonated beverage."

Jurgen got emotional as he took a swig of the beverage.

"Look," said Hans, "Jurgen is about to utter his first vord since ze incident."

Jurgen just let out a long belch instead.

"Oh, well," said Grampa. "It's a start!"

So, that's all there is. The police weren't as understanding as Dame Drenched and they threw Hans and Jurgen back into the funny farm.

Gramma was given a ticket for smuggling animals into the water park.

Jubal and I used the **C.R.U.D.** to make some cool new critters, like the Crawdaisy and the Craw-donut. Coming soon to a pet store near you.

As for the first toilet into space, witnesses say they saw it crash back to Earth last Wednes-day. . . .

Where it landed, no one is quite sure.

BEWARE!
BIG-
FOOT

Now there's a mega-budget movie about our crawdad adventure. Here are some exclusive photos from the red carpet premiere. Something's a little wacky with that second pic. Help us find the differences before we publish it in the *Hollyweird Reporter*.

The answers are on the back. Anyone caught cheating gets their head dunked in Mount Flushmore!

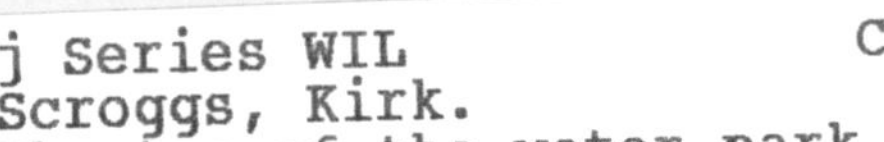


GHOST CHASERS
UP TO BAT
STEVEN SPILLBERG'S
CRAWS
RATED R RANCID
ARRRR!
ROTTEN REVIEW
BAZOOKA JOE
FLOWER POWER
DUCK!
SOUR PUSS
CLAWS
BATTY LASHES
CLAW TERROR
SPIKED DO
CLAWS 27
SEQUEL OPPORTUNITY
FACIAL SCARE
HAND OVER FOOT
TIE FIGHTER
ROBO BOY
LET'S HAVE A TOAST
NOW SHOWING
COMING SOON
DON'T GIMME NO LIP!
CHANGE THE CHANNEL
7
SNAKE HANDLER
SHAKEN, NOT STIRRED
FISHY
GETTING THE SCOOP
MEET THE BEETLE
SMILE
FUNNY BUNNY
WITH A FRIEND LIKE HAIRY
PET PRIDE
I ♥ MY